The Brown
Felt Hat

RICHARD TULLOCH

The Brown Felt Hat

Illustrated by Craig Smith

Young Piper Books
published by Pan Books

The author gratefully acknowledges the assistance of the
Literature Board of the Australia Council with this and
other projects.

First published 1990 by Omnibus Books, Australia
This Young Piper edition published 1991 by Pan Books Ltd,
Cavaye Place, London SW10 9PG

3 5 7 9 8 6 4

Text © Richard Tulloch 1990
Illustrations © Craig Smith 1990

ISBN 0 330 31931 0

Printed in England by Clays Ltd, St Ives plc

To Stephen, Charles and Paul

One day a hatmaker made a hat.

A wide-brimmed brown felt hat, decorated with bunches of dried flowers. It was a very elegant, very expensive hat.

The hatmaker was very pleased with it. "This hat is fit for a queen," he said. "This hat will really go places."

When it heard that, the brown felt hat swelled with pride, from size five-and-seven-eighths to size six-and-a-quarter. "Fit for a queen!" it thought. "Really go places! That means I'll travel the world and see the sights and meet all kinds of wonderful important people."

Sure enough, the next day the hat was bought by a rich lady—a tall, fashionable, well-dressed lady.

"Just the thing I was looking for!" she said. "This hat will match my brown handbag at the Spring Horse-racing Carnival."

"I knew it!" thought the brown felt hat. "Now I really am going places!"

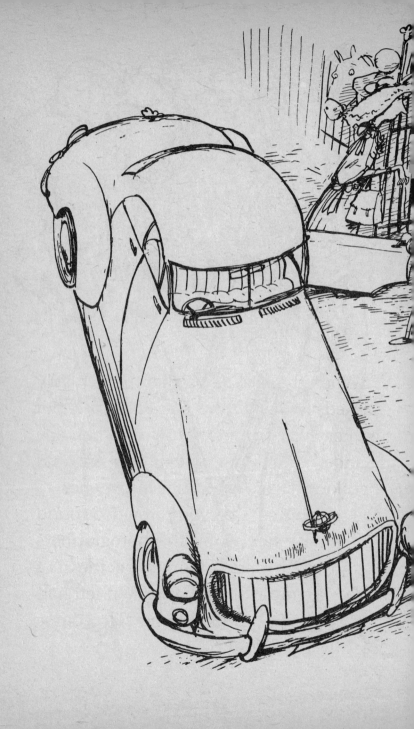

HORSES
MEMBERS
ONLY

When the race day came, the rich lady picked up her brown handbag and put on her wide-brimmed brown felt hat. She climbed into a long sleek limousine and her long sleek chauffeur drove her to the racecourse. Everyone crowded round to admire her clothes. Photographers fought with each other to be the first to photograph her in her brown felt hat. She won first prize at the Racecourse Fashion Parade.

The brown felt hat looked down on all the other hats, which were not so wide-brimmed and not so brown and didn't have bunches of dried flowers around their brims. It was so proud.

But the next day the rich lady bought a new handbag—a shiny blue handbag. The wide-brimmed brown felt hat didn't match it at all. So the rich lady bought a new shiny blue hat and gave the brown felt hat to her maid.

"Oh thank you, madam!" said the maid, giving a little curtsy. "It's just the thing I was looking for to wear to a picnic at the weekend."

"Great, just great!" thought the brown felt hat. "I'm a hat fit for a queen, I'm two weeks old, and already I'm a hand-me-down! How can I go places with a lady's maid?"

That Saturday, the maid put on the brown felt hat and she and her boyfriend drove out into the country and spread out a picnic blanket in a field.

The boyfriend told the maid he loved her brown felt hat, and he loved her, and she had never looked so beautiful. "Listen to the birds all twittering in the trees," he said. He was a pretty soppy boyfriend.

The soppy boyfriend tried to kiss the maid and the wide brim of the brown felt hat poked him in the eye. But the maid just giggled, took off the hat, and put it on the blanket beside her.

A gust of wind started to tug at the hat, but the maid didn't pay any attention because she was busy kissing her soppy boyfriend. A stronger gust of wind rolled the hat off the blanket, but the maid still didn't notice. She was so busy kissing her soppy boyfriend that she didn't even notice when the wind sent the hat bounding across the field, over the road and away down into the valley.

"Great, just g-g-great!" thought the brown felt hat, as it bounced up and down on the tufts of rough grass. "Is this any way to t-treat a hat fit for a queen?"

Then it landed in a lump of cow dung—SPLAT!

A few days later a farmer rode past on his horse and noticed the brown felt hat, which by now had blown up against a fence and got stuck on the barbed wire. He picked it up and examined it. He banged it on his knee to get the dust off.

"Just the thing I was looking for!" said
the farmer. "It's a bit battered, but I need
a wide-brimmed hat to keep the sun off."

First he pulled off the dried flowers.
(There was nothing soppy about the
farmer.) Then he tried the hat on his
head. It fitted perfectly.

The farmer wore the hat while he was working in the paddocks. He waved it at the sheep when he was rounding them up. He used it to wipe the sweat off his forehead on hot days. He put it over his enamel mug to keep the dust out of his tea.

"Great, just great!" thought the brown felt hat. "Here I am, a hat fit for a queen, being used like an ordinary tea cosy!"

Each day, when he finished work, the farmer used to hang the brown felt hat on a peg in his hayshed.

One night a dusty old swagman sneaked in to find a bed in the hay and noticed the hat.

His face was unshaven, and he had holes in his old grey overcoat and blanket and in the soles of his swagman's shoes.

"Just the thing I was looking for," said
the swagman. "This wide-brimmed hat
will keep the rain off my face when I'm
camping by a billabong."

Next morning he plonked the brown
felt hat on his head and went tramping
away along the dusty country tracks.

The swagman used the brown felt hat to fan his campfire when the wood was wet, and to scoop up water from the creeks and waterholes when he needed a drink. And sometimes, if his nose was runny, he used the brown felt hat to wipe it clean.

"Great, just great!" thought the brown felt hat. "A hat fit for a queen shouldn't be used like any old snot rag! I'm supposed to be really going places!"

One day, while the swagman was lying asleep under a bridge with the brown felt hat across his face, along came a dog with a black patch over one eye and a wicked grin on its face.

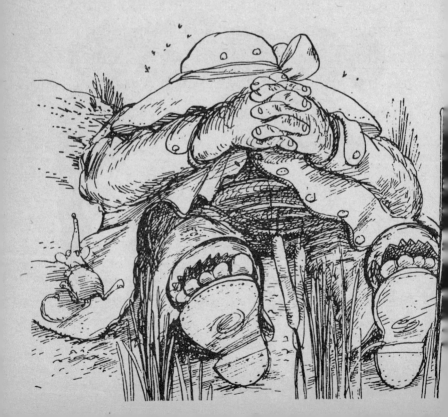

"Just the thing I was looking for!" said the dog. "I haven't found a rabbit to chase all day, but this smelly old brown felt hat will do me nicely." He grabbed the brown felt hat and ran away with it before the swagman could yell, "Come back here, you mongrel!"

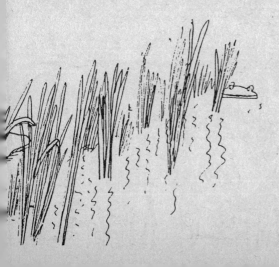

The dog tossed the brown felt hat this way and that. He dragged it into ditches and through a patch of mud. As the dog became hotter and more excited, the hat was stained with slobber from his floppy jaws.

"Great, just great," thought the brown felt hat. "This is no way to treat a hat fit for a queen. I'm supposed to be going places!"

The dog came to a creek and stopped for a drink. He dropped the hat into the water, and before he could pick it up again the current whipped it away.

All through the day the brown felt hat jumped through whirlpools and waterfalls, dodged sticks and snags and scooted over sandbanks until the creek turned into a river.

All through the night the hat floated down the river until the river flowed majestically out into the sea.

The brown felt hat sloshed around in the ocean until it was completely full of water. Then it started a new journey—sinking slowly downward towards the bottom.

A shark nibbled the edges of the hat, but decided that a nice fat mackerel would make a better meal.

A hermit crab made his home in it for a few days, but decided that a large shiny shell would make a better house for impressing his friends.

"Great, just . . . blub, blub . . . great!" said the brown felt hat. "I'm supposed to be a hat fit for a queen, and instead of going places I'm stuck at the bottom of the sea!"

For a long time after that the brown felt hat drifted around in the ocean.

Once a fisherman caught it with his hook and pulled it up to the surface, but when he saw it was only a brown felt hat he swore under his breath and threw it overboard again.

Once a shipwrecked sailor fished it out and used it to catch rainwater to drink. But when he was rescued by a passing ship he left the hat on his raft, because it brought back too many bad memories.

And so it drifted on and on, carried by the currents that play around the world's great oceans, tossed by the waves and the shifting tides until at last it was washed up on the clean white beach of a tropical island.

It lay half buried in the sand, steam rising from its wide brim as it dried in the sun.

"Just the thing I was looking for!" cried a shabby woman, poking the brown felt hat with a stick. "A hat fit for a queen!" And she took it to a rock pool and rinsed it and decorated it with a band of dried seaweed.

"Great, just great!" thought the brown felt hat. "As if I haven't had enough misery and disappointment in my life, now I've been captured by a crazy old beachcomber!"

A stiff young man in a neat white suit and uncomfortable leather shoes picked his way across the rocks and cleared his throat nervously.

"Er . . . ahem . . . Excuse me, your majesty, but don't you think we should be going? Your subjects will be expecting you back at the palace."

"All in good time, my man. A queen doesn't often get a holiday, and I mean to make the most of it."

The brown felt hat couldn't believe what it was hearing. The woman really *was* a queen!

"A very interesting hat, don't you think?" she was saying.

"Er . . . a bit . . . ahem . . . messy, your majesty," said the stiff young man.

"This is clearly a very special hat," continued the queen firmly. "It has personality, and that is something which even a queen can't buy in the most expensive store in the world. This hat has obviously been places."

"I could, er, wrap it in newspaper if your majesty wishes to take it back to the palace . . ."

"Certainly not," said the queen. "Life in a stuffy old palace would be far too dull for a hat with personality."

She laid the brown felt hat gently on a rock and walked slowly away up the beach.

That night, the tide came in and
covered the rock, and once again the
brown felt hat was washed out to sea.
But it didn't mind.

It was a hat fit for a queen, and it was
going places.

James Riordan
The Boy Who Turned Into a Goat £2.50
and other stories of magical changes

Catherine warned her brother not to drink the water in the forest. "For if you do," she said, "you will turn into a goat."

Boys like Sean rarely take notice of the things their sisters say – but, oh, how he wished he had!

Read about the fishermen who became crows, the princess who turned into an apple, the magical vinegar jar and other amazing tales of transformations from around the world!

Ideal for readers who are progressing from picture books to longer stories – and for reading aloud.

Eva Ibbotson
The Worm and the Toffee-Nosed Princess £1.99
and other stories of monsters

Why did the giant, hairy worm eat the snooty princess? What happened to
the silly dog who dared to annoy a Frid? And how did the three Scotsmen
deal with a sheep-eating Boobrie?

Find out the answers to these and other questions in this collection of
funny tales about monsters, written specially for readers who are
progressing from picture books to longer stories.

Ann Lawrence
Beyond the Firelight £1.99
and other stories of hobgoblins

Young Will looked after his farm, and hard work it was too. But one day a strange creature appeared and started to help out with the chores. At first Will was delighted, but his new wife wasn't so sure . . .

Boggarts, hobgoblins, fairies and magical creatures – they're all here in this delightful collection of stories that's ideal for reading aloud or for children to read on their own.

In Stitches with Ms Wiz £1.99

When Jack goes to hospital, he never thought it would be so weird – or so much fun!

There was a walking appendix, a plague of white mice and a stethoscope that played disco music!

Only a witch could be behind such side-splitting stunts. Her name is Ms Wiz. And she's back to tickle ribs and leave everyone in stitches!

Siân Lewis
The Saddlebag Hero £1.99

Lyn wanted an Alsatian for her tenth birthday. She wanted an Alsatian as big as herself with a terrifying growl: She wanted an Alsatian who'd scare the living daylights out of String, who sat behind her in class.

Lyn calls her new pet Alsatian even though he isn't really a dog at all. But he turns out to be quite a hero in his own – slightly smaller – way . . .

'A marvellously readable book'
Children's Books of the Year 1985

All Pan books are available at your local bookshop or newsagent, or can be ordered direct from the publisher. Indicate the number of copies required and fill in the form below.

Send to: **CS Department, Pan Books Ltd., P.O. Box 40, Basingstoke, Hants. RG21 2YT.**

or phone: 0256 469551 (Ansaphone), quoting title, author and Credit Card number.

Please enclose a remittance* to the value of the cover price plus: 60p for the first book plus 30p per copy for each additional book ordered to a maximum charge of £2.40 to cover postage and packing.

*Payment may be made in sterling by UK personal cheque, postal order, sterling draft or international money order, made payable to Pan Books Ltd.

Alternatively by Barclaycard/Access:

Card No.

Signature:

Applicable only in the UK and Republic of Ireland.

While every effort is made to keep prices low, it is sometimes necessary to increase prices at short notice. Pan Books reserve the right to show on covers and charge new retail prices which may differ from those advertised in the text or elsewhere.

NAME AND ADDRESS IN BLOCK LETTERS PLEASE:

Name————————————————————————

Address———————————————————————